Lord of the Flies

Lightbox Literature Studies

Blaine Wiseman

LIGHTBOX
openlightbox.com

LIGHTBOX

Go to
www.openlightbox.com
and enter this book's
unique code.

ACCESS CODE

LBK42537

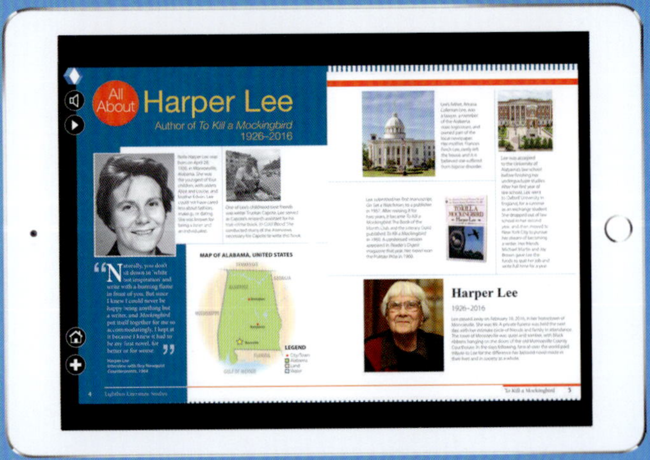

Lightbox is an all-inclusive digital solution for the teaching and learning of curriculum topics in an original, groundbreaking way. Lightbox is based on National Curriculum Standards.

STANDARD FEATURES OF LIGHTBOX

AUDIO High-quality narration using text-to-speech system

VIDEOS Embedded high-definition video clips

ACTIVITIES Printable PDFs that can be emailed and graded

WEBLINKS Curated links to external, child-safe resources

SLIDESHOWS Pictorial overviews of key concepts

TRANSPARENCIES Step-by-step layering of maps, diagrams, charts, and timelines

INTERACTIVE MAPS Interactive maps and aerial satellite imagery

QUIZZES Ten multiple choice questions that are automatically graded and emailed for teacher assessment

KEY WORDS Matching key concepts to their definitions

MORE Extra information and details on the subject

FIRST HAND Letters, diaries, and other primary sources

DOCS Speeches, newspaper articles, and other historical documents

Contents

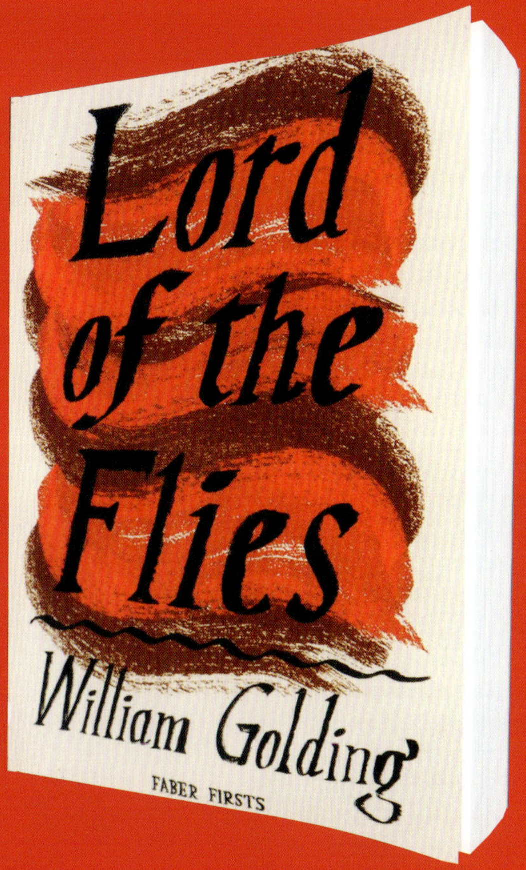

EXTENSION ACTIVITY

Holding a Classroom Debate

Students will form groups and prepare arguments for a debate on a controversial issue. Exemplary performance in a debate will meet the following criteria.

- Demonstrates in-depth understanding of the topic and related information
- Presents strong, logical, and convincing arguments
- Communicates in a clear and confident manner
- Maintains eye contact
- Uses clear vocal tone and a reasonable rate of vocal delivery
- Uses respectful and appropriate language and body language
- Delivers arguments, evidence, and counter-evidence in an engaging and persuasive manner
- Supports each major point of an argument with several relevant and detailed facts and examples
- Connects all arguments to the overall topic in a clear, concise, and organized manner
- Presents the arguments and supporting evidence in a clear, logical manner
- Presents clear, thorough, and accurate information throughout the debate
- Addresses all of the opposing team's arguments with counter-arguments
- Identifies any weakness in the opposing team's arguments
- Constructs strong and relevant counter-arguments using accurate information
- Presents strong and persuasive arguments throughout the debate
- Summarizes the arguments in the closing statement

All About

William Golding

Author of *Lord of the Flies*
1911–1993

Sir William Gerald Golding is one of the twentieth century's most celebrated authors. He is best known for his classic novel, *Lord of the Flies*. Golding wrote 12 novels, along with several plays, poems, essays, articles, and a travel book.

Golding was born on September 19, 1911, in the village of Saint Columb Minor, near Southern England's Cornwall coast. His father was headmaster of a grammar school and his mother was a **suffragette**.

"A novel ensures that we can look before and after, take action at whatever pace we choose, read again and again, skip and go back. The story in a book is humble and serviceable, available, friendly, is not switched on and off but taken up and put down, lasts a lifetime. … There is no other medium in which we can live for so long and so intimately with a character. That is the service a novel renders."

William Golding,
Nobel Lecture

MAP OF THE UNITED KINGDOM

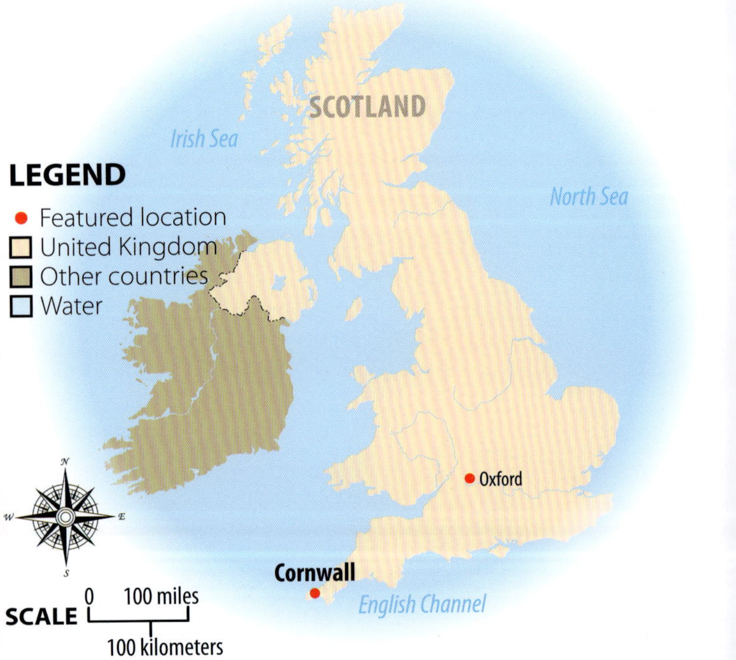

World War I was the major event in Golding's early life. Local men went to war, while women worked in factories. British ships battled German submarines off the coast. The war helped Golding develop a sense of patriotism, while showing him humanity's dark side.

After grammar school, Golding continued his studies at Oxford University. His father hoped he would become a scientist, but William wanted to be a writer. He studied English Literature at Oxford's Brasenose College. Golding's publishing career began even before he graduated. In 1934, he published his first book of poetry.

After graduating from Brasenose, Golding worked briefly in the theater as an actor and writer. Soon after, he decided to follow his father into the teaching profession. Teaching English and philosophy at a school for young boys gave Golding a great deal of inspiration for his first novel. However, he would leave teaching to join the fight in World War II. For nearly six years, Golding sailed with the British Navy.

When the war ended, Golding returned to the classroom, and also worked on his writing career. In 1954, Golding finally published his first novel. *Lord of the Flies* became an instant classic, and kickstarted a career that would earn him awards and admiration all over the world. Queen Elizabeth II knighted him Sir William Golding in 1988. He died in Cornwall in 1993.

TEACHER NOTES

Google Maps

University of Oxford, Oxford, United Kingdom

Explore the university campus William Golding attended using street view.

Weblink

Changing Lives: Gender Expectations and Roles during and after World War One

Examine the British Library article discussing gender roles in WWI.

1. To what degree did traditional gender roles change as a result of WWI? What lasting impacts do those changes have on society today? Justify your responses with evidence.
2. Based on your knowledge of Golding, what opinion might he have about the changes in gender roles that occurred as a result of WWI? Why?
3. For what reasons might a male with pacifist views during WWI have his masculinity questioned? How have perspectives on male pacifism changed today?

EXTENSION ACTIVITY

Analyzing a Newspaper Article

Students will assess a newspaper article and write an analysis. An exemplary analysis will meet the following criteria.

- Identifies the topic of the article
- Identifies the main points and opinions presented in the article
- Identifies the writer of the article
- Presents information about the writer and infers how his or her life may have shaped this opinion
- Assesses the writer's reliability
- Analyzes how the writer makes his or her argument
- Uses evidence from the article to show how the writer supports his or her argument
- Analyzes the writer's use of literary devices to enhance the article
- Differentiates between the facts and opinions presented in the article
- Identifies when and where the article was published, and determines its intended audience
- Identifies and understands the goals of the article
- Assesses the effectiveness of the format (a newspaper opinion article) in presenting the writer's argument
- Connects the article to the societal and historical context in which it was written
- Infers what is not said about this topic in the article
- Identifies what information is unintentionally implied in the article
- Infers what other opinions may be presented about this topic and who may be most likely to express them
- Uses a number of other resources to analyze the context of the article

Setting of the Novel

Lord of the Flies begins with Ralph and Piggy making their way through a jungle. Their airplane has crashed on an island somewhere in the Pacific Ocean. Three boys hike to the top of a nearby mountain to survey their surroundings from every direction. They see no smoke from fires and there is water all around them. This sight confirms their greatest hopes and fears. They are stranded on a deserted island. There are no other people besides the 30 boys who survived the plane crash. The boys are forced to form their own civilization from scratch.

Snapshot

There are more than **25,000 islands** in the Pacific Ocean.

Nauru, the **smallest island nation in the world**, covers **8 square miles** in the Pacific. (21 square kilometers)

Juana Maria, the **"Lone Woman of San Nicholas,"** spent **18 years** alone on an island off the coast of California. Her story inspired the classic castaway book, *Island of the Blue Dolphins*.

A Deserted Island

"They had guessed before that this was an island: clambering among the pink rocks, with the sea on either side, and the crystal heights of air, they had known by some instinct that the sea lay on every side. But there seemed something more fitting in leaving the last word till they stood on the top, and could see a circular horizon of water.
Ralph turned to the others.
'This belongs to us.'
It was roughly boat shaped: humped near this end with behind them the jumbled descent to the shore. On either side rocks, cliffs, tree-tops and a steep slope: forward there, the length of the boat, a tamer descent, tree-clad, with hints of pink: and then the jungly flat of the island, dense green, but drawn at the end to a pink tail. There, where the island petered out in water, was another island; a rock, almost detached, standing like a fort, facing them across the green with one bold, pink **bastion**."

Chapter One – The Sound of the Shell

William Golding's years at sea gave him plenty of inspiration for his novels. He sailed past, and into, many islands and foreign lands. The setting of *Lord of the Flies* is based on some of the scenery he saw during his travels. The imagery of towering mountains, dense jungles, sandy beaches, jagged reefs, and blue waters are inspired by his voyages at sea.

The boys' actions and reactions to the setting are based upon the actions and reactions of the world during the turbulent times in which Golding lived. The island society serves as a representation of the politics and society that created two world wars and the possibility of nuclear war. Given their isolation and primal setting, the boys have the opportunity to create their own society. As the novel progresses, the situation becomes increasingly ominous.

TEACHER NOTES

Video

***Lord of the Flies* (1990)**

Analyze the setting created by the 1990 film adaptation of *Lord of the Flies.*

1. Which elements of the set design and costuming are most effective in the portrayal of the setting of *Lord of the Flies*, as it appears in the novel? Which elements of the set design and costuming feel inconsistent or ineffective? In what ways? Provide reasons for your opinions.
2. Is this film adaptation consistent with the tone generated by the setting in the novel? Why or why not?

Weblink

***Lord of the Flies* Is Still a Blueprint for Savagery**

Examine the article from *The Independent* discussing real-life scenarios that mirror the events that transpire in the book.

1. Why might groups of survivors resort to savagery in the wake of disaster? In your opinion, is savagery innate, or is it the result of an evil presence or "beast"? Explain your responses.
2. Why does Golding's tale seem to suggest that the strong should not waste resources on the weak? What might be the intended effect of this suggestion?
3. If the island is a metaphor for the history of government, what can be inferred about Golding's view of humanity's ability to govern itself? Justify your position.

EXTENSION ACTIVITY

Analyzing a Political Cartoon

Students will complete an analysis of a political comic or cartoon. An exemplary analysis will meet the following criteria.

- Identifies the cartoonist and source publication
- Describes the target audience of the cartoon
- Makes note of any titles or captions in the cartoon
- Outlines any individuals or institutions that appear in the cartoon
- Identifies symbols found in the cartoon and determines their meaning
- Notes the most important phrases or words used by the cartoonist
- Infers the emotions that the cartoonist is portraying or evoking
- Interprets and explains the message of the cartoon
- Records the different persuasive techniques used by the cartoonist
- Identifies how different groups would respond to the cartoon's message
- Presents information in a clear, concise manner
- Uses correct spelling, grammar, and punctuation

Time Period of the Novel

Lord of the Flies takes place around the time it was written—the early 1950s. World War II had ended fewer than 10 years earlier. The United States had dropped two atomic bombs on Japan. Tension between the world's superpowers was growing, and the **Cold War** was underway. With countries racing to build and stockpile nuclear weapons, nuclear war seemed like a real possibility.

Nuclear War

"'How does he know we're here?'
Because, thought Ralph, because, because. The roar from the reef became very distant.
'They'd tell him at the airport.'
Piggy shook his head, put on his flashing glasses, and looked down at Ralph.
'Not them. Didn't you hear what the pilot said? About the atom bomb? They're all dead.'"

Chapter One – The Sound of the Shell

William Golding based his story in a world where nuclear war has already broken out. The nationalistic, warrior-like attitudes of the boys are both a product of the time period in which they were living, and a product of human nature.

British schoolboys in the early 1950s were familiar with death and destruction. During World War II, cities and towns around Britain were heavily damaged by enemy bombs. A British child who was 13 years old in 1954 would likely remember air raids and bomb shelters. Most would have lost family or friends, either in the bombing at home, or in the war overseas. Approximately 357,000 citizens of the United Kingdom were killed during the war, including 92,673 **civilians**.

Nations around the world developed nuclear programs to build their own atomic bombs. The United States and the former Soviet Union led the way, expanding their nuclear programs, and their powers. The Cold War would leave the world on the brink of nuclear war for decades to come.

TEACHER NOTES

First Hand

A Schoolboy's View of World War Two

Assess the accounts of a British schoolboy during World War II.

1. How would you describe the tone of this piece? How might an adult write about these same experiences?
2. What reasons might the boy in the article have had for thinking elements of the war were a game? How does his mentality compare with the that of the boys in the novel? Give specific examples from the text.

Document

"Peace Today" Political Cartoon

Analyze a 1948 Pulitzer Prize-winning political cartoon by Rube Goldberg.

1. What is Goldberg suggesting about the state of world peace during the Cold War? How effective is the cartoon in its depiction of the state of the world at the time? Why do you think so?
2. How effective is the kind of peace depicted in the cartoon? In your opinion, was the advent of the atomic bomb a step toward greater global stability or away from it? Justify your position.

EXTENSION ACTIVITY

Writing a Short Story

Students will choose an excerpt from the novel and use it as their inspiration in writing a short story. An exemplary short story will meet the following criteria.

- Engages the reader from the opening line
- Establishes a clear, consistent point of view
- Introduces a narrator and a setting
- Develops an engaging conflict at the heart of the narrative to build tension and keep the reader interested
- Develops characters and events through purposeful and well-crafted literary devices
- Creates a logical progression of events in the narrative that build upon each other using various techniques
- Explores ideas, concepts, and writing styles with creativity and originality
- Demonstrates a high level of skill in using appropriate narrative techniques to tell the story
- Concludes the narrative in a thoughtful, effective manner appropriate to the narrative
- Uses varied, purposeful diction and syntax to affect style and serve the narrative
- Writes with clarity, imagination, and a unique, personal voice
- Does not use stereotypes or clichés
- Uses effective, believable dialogue
- Uses correct spelling, grammar, and punctuation

Conflict in the Novel

Conflict is a constant source of drama in *Lord of the Flies*. It is conflict that puts the boys on the island to begin with, and they struggle against their new environment. Almost immediately, conflict between the characters begins to grow. As the story progresses, the boys' own conflicting emotions and beliefs grow as well. The four types of conflict in literature are character vs. character, character vs. nature, character vs. self, and character vs. society. Great stories feature one or more of these conflict types. Talented writers such as William Golding are able to use all four conflict types to create drama, suspense, and action.

CHARACTER VS. CHARACTER

When two or more characters struggle against one another, it can create a memorable story. Many classic war, sports, and race stories include major character vs. character conflicts. *Treasure Island* by Robert Louis Stevenson features a race between Jim, the protagonist, and Long John Silver, the antagonist, to uncover buried treasure.

CHARACTER VS. SELF

A common type of conflict in coming-of-age stories is character versus self. When a character struggles with emotional, mental, or moral issues, it often leads to growth in that character. One of the major conflicts in *The Outsiders* by S.E. Hinton features Ponyboy, who struggles with issues of maturity when he is no longer a child, but not yet a man.

CHARACTER VS. SOCIETY

Many great novels have been written as a critique of the writer's society. Utopian and dystopian novels, tales of rebellion, and political stories often feature characters struggling against their culture, community, or leaders. In *Island*, Aldous Huxley creates conflict between his characters and a fictional utopian society. Outside influences threaten the traditions and lifestyles of the Palanese people.

CHARACTER VS. NATURE

A character often battles against natural elements in tales of survival and adventure. Weather, animals, and disease can all cause character versus nature conflict. *Robinson Crusoe* by Daniel Defoe is a classic of English literature that features a protagonist struggling to survive in a harsh environment. In his voyages, Crusoe survives shipwrecks, storms, illnesses, animal attacks, and many other struggles.

Types of Conflict in *Lord of the Flies*

Character versus Society

"'The rules!' shouted Ralph, 'you're breaking the rules!'
'Who cares?'
Ralph summoned his wits.
'Because the rules are the only thing we've got!'
But Jack was shouting against him.
'Bollocks to the rules! We're strong – we hunt! If there's a beast, we'll hunt it down! We'll close in and beat and beat and beat – !'"

Chapter Five – Beast from Water

Character versus Character

"They walked along, two continents of experience and feeling, unable to communicate.
'If I could only get a pig!'
'I'll come back and go on with the shelter.'
They looked at each other, baffled, in love and hate. All the warm salt water of the bathing-pool and the shouting and splashing and laughing were only just sufficient to bring them together again."

Chapter Three – Huts on the Beach

Character versus Self

"Now that his physical voice was silent the inner voice of reason, and other voices too, made themselves heard. Piggy was calling him a kid. Another voice told him not to be a fool; and the darkness and desperate enterprise gave the night a kind of dentist's chair unreality."

Chapter Seven – Shadows and Tall Trees

Character versus Nature

"They lay there listening, at first with doubt but then with terror to the description the twins breathed at them between bouts of extreme silence. Soon the darkness was full of claws, full of the awful unknown and menace. An interminable dawn faded the stars out, and at last light, sad and grey, filtered into the shelter. They began to stir though still the world outside the shelter was impossibly dangerous."

Chapter Six – Beast from Air

TEACHER NOTES

More

The Types of Conflict in *Lord of the Flies*

Analyze the citations from the novel revealing the types of conflict as they appear in *Lord of the Flies.*

1. How do these excerpts of conflict reveal the novel's theme? How do they reveal character? Explain and defend your ideas.
2. Write an analysis of Golding's development of conflict between Jack and Ralph. What deeper truths may be suggested about these characters as a result of their conflict?

Weblink

Why Writers Treasure Islands

Examine the article from *The Guardian* about why writers find islands to be a rich, dramatic platform for fiction.

1. What makes an island the perfect setting for the conflicts in *Lord of the Flies* to unfold? How does the island, as a character, contribute to the rising conflict in the novel?
2. How might present perspectives influence how a reader today interprets the character versus nature conflict of being stranded on an island? Would this strengthen or diminish the power of Golding's allegory? Why?

EXTENSION ACTIVITY

Researching for a Writing Assignment

Students will complete a thorough research process to prepare for a writing assignment, and organize their research in a logical manner that supports their writing. An exemplary research process will meet the following criteria.

- Creates a goal for the research, based on the topic and working thesis
- Creates specific, thoughtful, and inventive research questions that are relevant to the topic of the writing assignment
- Produces a list of categories, key words, and related ideas to effectively assist in researching
- Uses high-quality sources that pertain to the topic and come in a variety of formats, such as books, journals, primary sources, websites, and databases
- Determines accuracy of all sources
- Uses sources that provide balanced research and various perspectives on the topic in question
- Takes notes to highlight the key facts and ideas in order to answer all research questions
- Extracts relevant, detailed information from the sources during the note-taking process
- Organizes the research notes in a clear and concise manner
- Organizes the research notes logically and in a way that sets up the information and ideas for analysis and the writing process
- Analyzes the information and produces ideas and points to support the working thesis
- Uses an effective and suitable format to present all research
- Properly cites all sources used

Introducing the Characters

The most celebrated stories in literature usually feature memorable characters. The actions and reactions, words, situations, motivations, thoughts, beliefs, and values are revealed to the reader as the story unfolds. Golding created an incredibly memorable cast of characters in *Lord of the Flies*. Each major character has his own unique character traits that move the story along.

Major Characters in *Lord of the Flies*

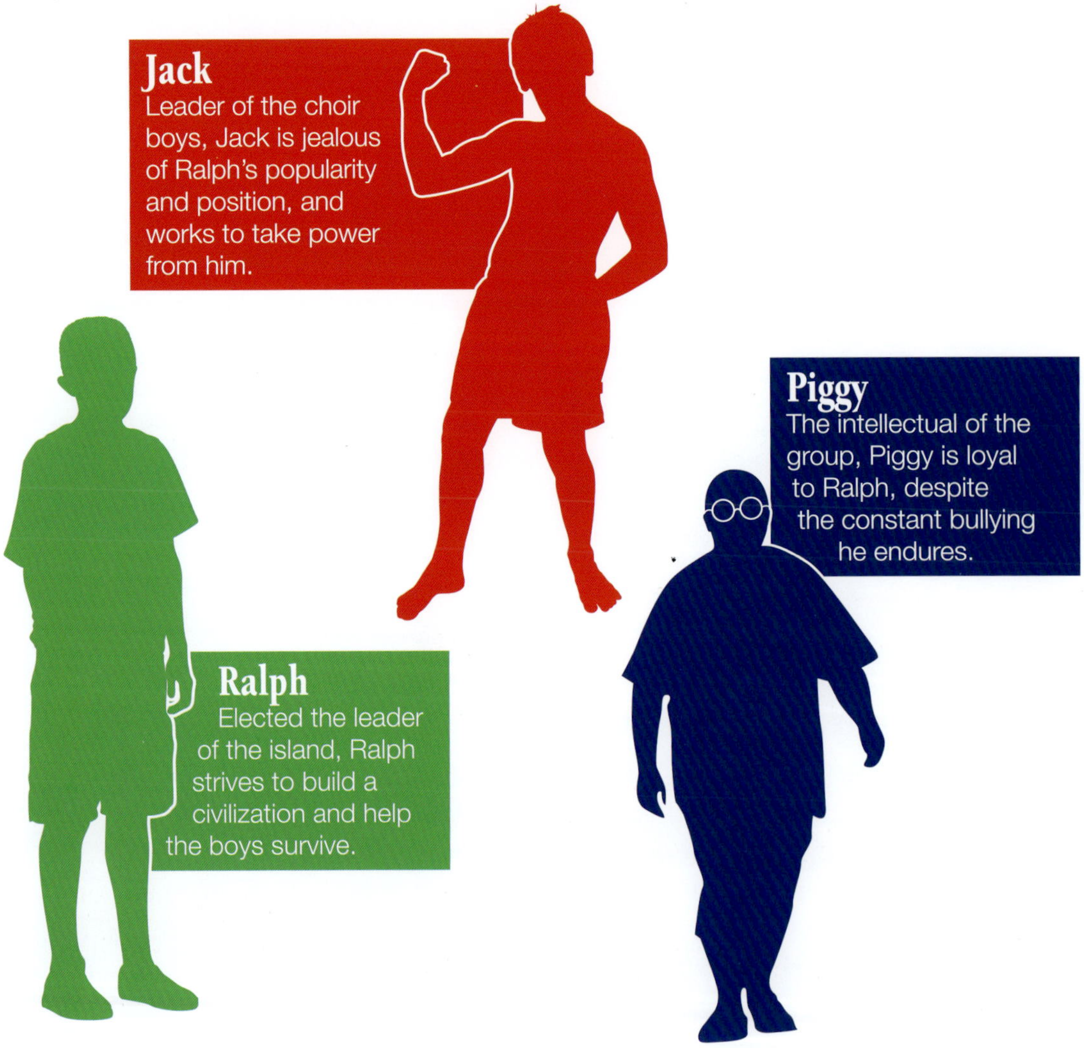

The characters in *Lord of the Flies* were inspired by Golding's familiarity with the natural behavior of boys. He had read plenty of boys' adventure stories featuring one-dimensional characters. These characters were kind, thoughtful, smart, heroic, and brave. Golding wanted to write a story that showed how boys truly behave. Jealousy, cowardice, anger, fear, and hatred were some of the traits he hoped to show.

Ralph is the protagonist in *Lord of the Flies*. He is **charismatic**, thoughtful, brave, and principled. These characteristics make him an ideal leader. The antagonist, Jack, is another charismatic leader, who gains power gradually. As the boys descend from civilization to savagery, Jack's **authoritative** nature helps him control the group.

There are many supporting characters who each offer something unique to the story. Some, such as Piggy and Simon, are very well-developed. The reader gets to know and understand these characters. Other minor characters are less developed, but still important to the story. For example, the littluns remain mostly unknown to readers individually, but as a group, they play a major role in the story.

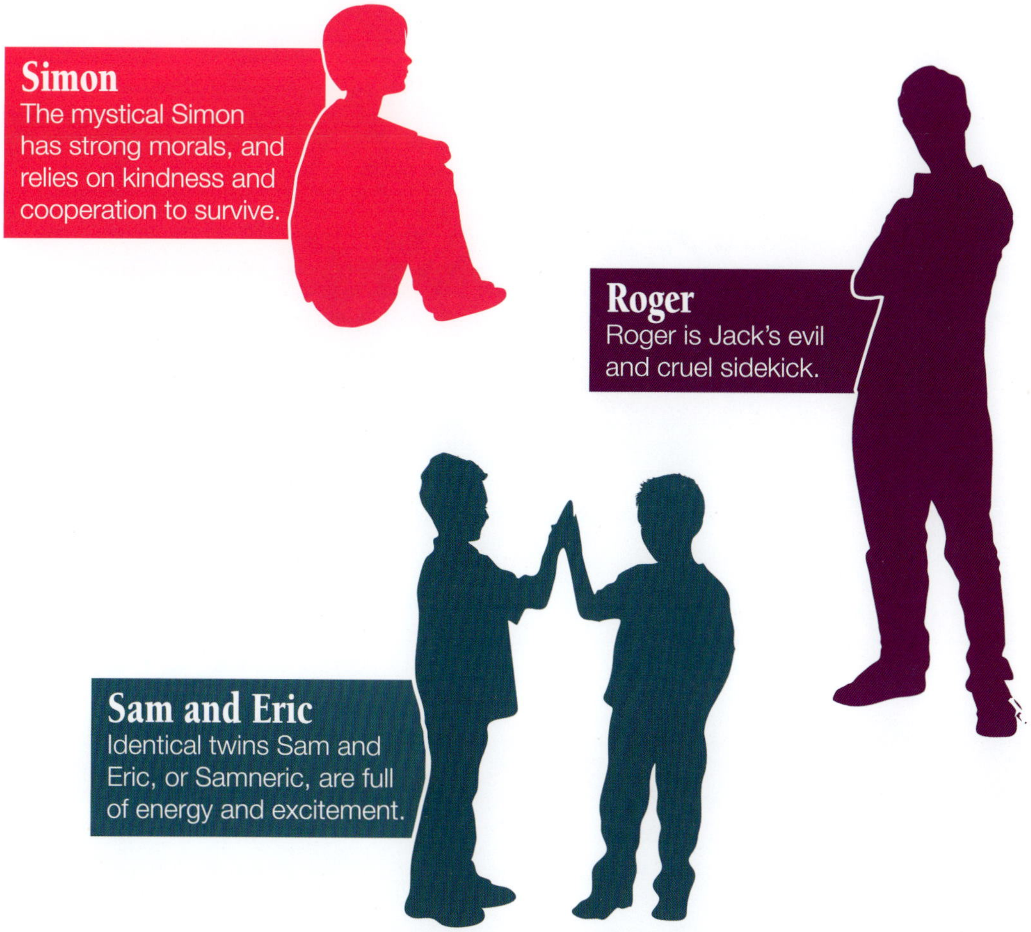

TEACHER NOTES

Video

William Golding Talks about *Lord of the Flies*

Examine the illustrated video interview of William Golding discussing one of his most famous works.

1. Are Golding's reasons for not using female characters justified? Why or why not?
2. How important was it for Golding to use males instead of females for this particular story? How would the story change if the characters were all female? How might it work if there was a mix of male and female characters? Explain and defend your responses in a short essay.

More

Character Development in *Lord of the Flies*

Analyze the characters in *Lord of the Flies* using the descriptions on the character map and excerpts from each character. Then, choose a character and answer the following questions.

1. Which of the writer's techniques are most effective at revealing this character's traits? Why?
2. In what ways is the characterization of this character ineffective? What could be done to improve this character's function in the novel? Defend your ideas with evidence.

EXTENSION ACTIVITY

Creating a Literary Device Analysis Booklet

Students will analyze the author's use of a literary device in the novel, and create a booklet to present this analysis. An exemplary literary device analysis booklet will meet the following criteria.

- Defines the chosen literary device accurately and in detail
- Places the definition of the literary device at the beginning of the booklet
- Provides strong, specific examples of how this literary device is used in the novel
- Describes examples in detail, with quotations properly integrated
- Includes thorough analysis of the use, purpose, and effectiveness of each example of how the chosen literary device is used in the novel
- Arranges all pages logically
- Examples are organized chronologically
- Provides no more than one example and its analysis per page
- Creates a neat, well-organized, and attractive booklet
- Booklet is colorful and displays the student's creativity
- Uses illustrations to represent the chosen literary device and the examples of how it is used in the novel

The Art of Storytelling

In *Lord of the Flies*, Golding tells a compelling story of survival. He uses literary techniques and elements to create suspense, drama, mystery, and action. These tools help keep readers interested in the story. Golding uses literary devices to narrate the conflicts in the story, and to show the growth and changes happening within and between the characters.

Structure of a Narrative

Lord of the Flies follows the most commonly-used narrative structure in literature. The novel features a beginning, a middle, and an end. In the beginning, the author introduces the characters and the situation in which they find themselves. The middle of the story builds toward a climax. This is the rising action. In the end, the story comes to a conclusion, in which the falling action results in a resolution.

Freytag's Pyramid

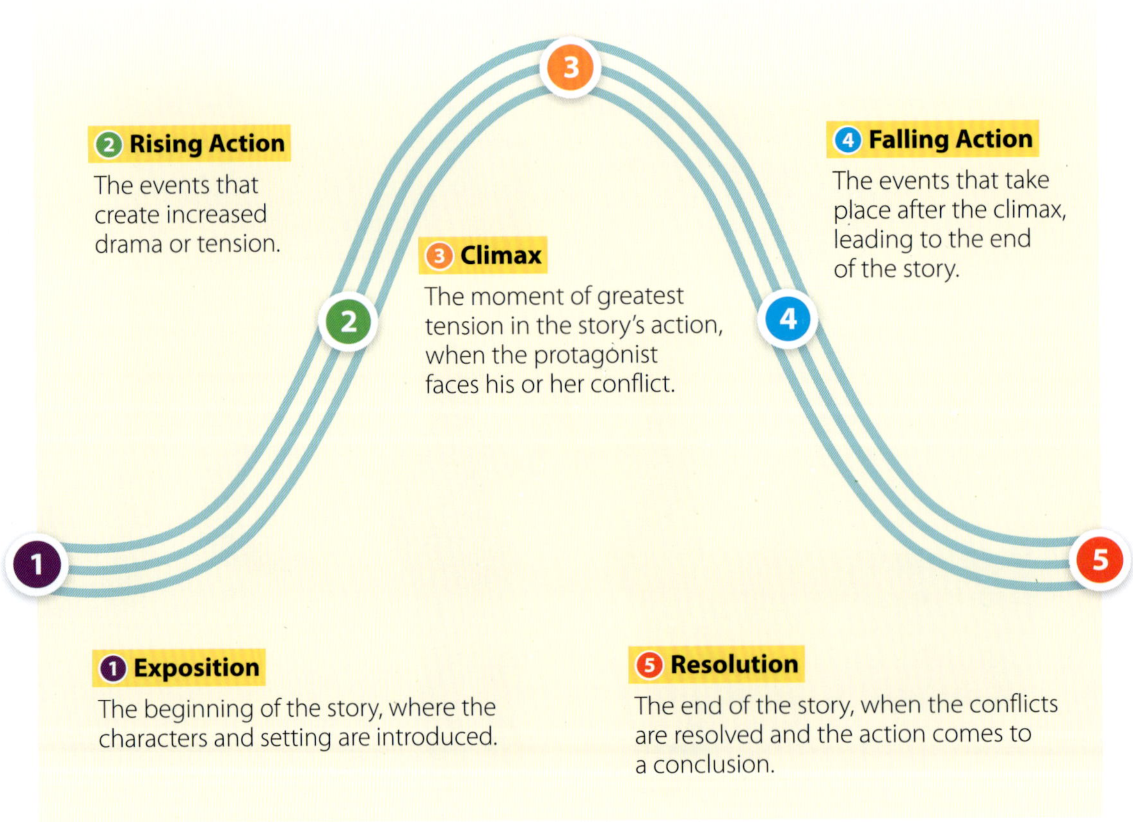

Plot

A story's plot is what puts the sequence of events together. It is the collection of actions and occurrences in the story. The linear plot of *Lord of the Flies* introduces readers to each plot point chronologically, as they unfold. Linear plots create a timeline along which the plot occurs.

Plot Points in Chapter Eight of *Lord of the Flies*

1. Ralph, Jack, and Roger tell the others they saw the beast.
2. Jack proposes a vote to remove Ralph from the role of Chief.
3. When no one supports his vote, Jack leaves the group.
4. Several boys follow Jack into the forest. Ralph, Piggy, and others build a new signal fire.
5. Jack and his group savagely kill a sow.
6. Jack's group tempt the rest of the boys with the offer of a feast.
7. Simon sits in his secret hiding spot and stares at the pig's head.
8. Simon hallucinates, thinking the Lord of the Flies is talking to him.

Literary Devices

Authors create dynamic stories using literary devices. Literary devices are the unique elements of a narrative that capture a reader's imagination and take them deeper into the story.

Literary Elements

A literary element is a feature of a narrative that appears in almost every work of literature. The narrative needs these major features in order to be effective and engaging.

- **Mood**: The atmosphere or overall feeling of a story.
- **Protagonist**: The main character or the character who provides the moral compass of a story.
- **Setting**: The place in which a story occurs.

Literary Techniques

Literary techniques are the various ways a writer can manipulate language to convey meaning or to create a distinct style.

- **Personification**: Giving human characteristics or traits to non-human forces, items, or characters.
- **Foreshadowing**: Hinting at an event that will take place later in a story.
- **Allusion**: Referencing classic literature, folklore, or stories without actually mentioning them.

TEACHER NOTES

Weblink

William Golding Says Author's Style Will Change with Subject Matter

Examine the article from the February 21, 1963 edition of *The Harvard Crimson*, highlighting a discussion with William Golding about writing style.

1. In what ways is Golding's commentary on writing style valid? Is it inevitable that a writer's style will change based on the subject matter of his or her work? Why do you think so?
2. If what Golding says about a writer having a distinct style is true, what is the corollary? What might Golding's differing descriptions of water in *Lord of the Flies* suggest about his style in this novel? Support your ideas with examples from the text.

More

Examples of Literary Techniques from the Novel

Analyze the author's use of literary techniques and how they contribute to the narrative of *Lord of the Flies*.

1. Choose one literary technique used in the novel. In what particular way did the author use this literary technique? How effective was its usage?
2. What arguments can be made for the use of your chosen literary technique in a text? If this technique were overused or underutilized, what effect might it have on an author's work?

Theme in the Novel

Every story has a theme. A theme is a message or meaning contained within a story. Most stories have multiple themes. As the events of a story unfold, the author's opinions, questions, thoughts, and desires are revealed. When one theme is evident throughout a work, it is considered a major theme. Minor themes can appear briefly or intermittently as a story unfolds.

Values

An author's values are often reflected in the themes presented in his or her work. Writers create characters with values that either match or clash with their own values. The words, actions, and reactions of these characters reveal their own values, as well as those of the author.

Major Themes of *Lord of the Flies*

One major theme explored throughout *Lord of the Flies* is civilization. **Marooned** on the island, the boys are forced to develop their own society, or civilization, from scratch. What begins as a civilized community built on rules and cooperation quickly deteriorates into a chaotic, uncivilized world of violence and fear.

Ralph

Civilization

"Supposing they could be transported home by jet, then before morning they would land at that big airfield in Wiltshire. They would go by car; no, for things to be perfect they would go by train; all the way down to Devon and take that cottage again. Then at the foot of the garden the wild ponies would come and look over the wall.
Ralph turned relentlessly in the leaves. Dartmoor was wild and so were the ponies. But the attraction of wildness had gone."

Chapter Ten – The Shell and the Glasses

Simon

Good and Evil

"The tide swelled in over the rain-pitted sand and smoothed everything with a layer of silver. Now it touched the first of the stains that seeped from the broken body and the creatures made a moving patch of light as they gathered at the edge. The water rose further and dressed Simon's coarse hair with brightness. The line of his cheek silvered and the turn of his shoulder became sculptured marble."

Chapter Nine – A View to a Death

Jack

Individualism

"The hands that held the conch shook. He cleared his throat, and spoke loudly.
'All right then.'
… The humiliating tears were running from the corner of each eye.
… Jack cleared his throat again.
'I'm not going to be part of Ralph's lot – '
He looked along the right-hand logs, numbering the hunters that had been a choir.
'I'm going off by myself. He can catch his own pigs. Anyone who wants to hunt when I do can come too.'

Chapter Eight – Gift for the Darkness

Secondary Themes

Minor themes add levels of analysis to a story. While deserving of exploration on their own, they also add depth to set up further investigation of the major theme. In *Lord of the Flies*, the reader explores the major theme by inspecting minor themes such as innocence, leadership, and **ritualism**.

TEACHER NOTES

First Hand

William Golding: A Frighteningly Honest Writer

Evaluate the article by author Nigel Williams on his memories of working with William Golding.

1. In your opinion, how do the themes explored in *Lord of the Flies* connect with Golding's desire "to explore the evolution of society, from chaos to collective action"? Defend your position with evidence from the novel.
2. Do the themes discussed in *Lord of the Flies* contribute to a "critical look at our history"? Why or why not? How are these themes connected to history?

More

Major and Secondary Themes

Analyze the author's development of themes over the course of the novel.

1. Choose a secondary theme from this spread and analyze its appearances in the novel. How does this theme first emerge? Which is the most poignant example of this theme in the novel?
2. What particular commentary might the author be making about life as a result of this theme's presence in the text?
3. Choose a major theme presented on pages 16–17. In what ways does your chosen secondary theme relate to this major theme? Does it deepen or detract from the major theme? How or in what way?

Symbolism in the Novel

Authors use symbols to create meaning in their stories. Themes have a greater impact on readers when presented using symbolism, rather than simple explanations. Some symbols are obvious, while others are less apparent. Analyzing symbols in a work of literature creates a meaningful connection between the reader, the story, and the author.

Lord of the Flies is filled with symbolism. The first major symbol introduced in the novel is the conch shell that Piggy and Ralph find on the beach. The sound of the shell brings all the boys together and it is then used to keep order during meetings. This is an obvious symbol of civilization. In the same scene, the author introduces Jack and the choir boys. With their uniform dress, leader, and strict rules of behavior, these boys are a symbol of **militarism**. They come to represent the bloodlust and frenzied patriotism of a nation at war.

The Beast

"'We'll kill a pig and give a feast.' He paused and went on more slowly. 'And about the beast. When we kill we'll leave some of the kill for it. Then it won't bother us, maybe.'"

Chapter Eight – Gift for the Darkness

The Beast as a Symbol

The beast is an unseen thing that is said to lurk in the darkness of the forest, hunting the boys. Fear of the beast gradually grows until it becomes a major focus. In the end, the author reveals that the beast is not a real creature, but a natural force dwelling within each of the boys. It is the savage instinct that has led the boys towards violence and evil. The beast characterizes savagery, evil, and fear.

Savagery It does not take long for the boys to become as **uninhibited** and wild as the island on which they find themselves.

Evil Without rules or morals, the boys become a mob driven by bloodlust and hate. Chaos rules until they are reminded of their morals and civility at the end of the novel.

Fear Much like society during wartime or heated political campaigns, the boys are driven by fear. They imagine a beast lurking in the dark, but deep down, they are truly afraid of the beast within themselves.

EXTENSION ACTIVITY

Creating a Symbolism Poster

Students will choose one of the other symbols listed on page 19 and analyze its role in the novel. They will then create a poster to present their analysis. An exemplary symbolism poster will meet the following criteria.

- Presents a clear purpose that is conveyed throughout the poster
- Shows an understanding of the concept of symbolism and the role it plays in the novel
- Provides an in-depth analysis of what the symbol represents
- Discusses the role the symbol plays in the novel
- Clearly indicates where the symbol appears in the novel
- Uses specific, detailed examples from the text to support the analysis
- Makes clear connections to the text
- Properly integrates all quotations
- Organizes the information in a logical, easy-to-read manner
- Includes high-quality graphics that relate to the symbol and effectively enhance understanding of the topic
- Features clear and concise writing
- Uses correct spelling, grammar, and punctuation
- Clearly labels items of importance
- Headings and subheadings are clear and easy to read
- Uses layout to creatively enhances the information
- Creates a poster that is attractive in terms of layout, design, and organization
- Shows a strong effort by the student

Who Is the Beast?

Other Symbols in the Novel

The Glasses

Piggy's glasses symbolize science and knowledge. They display Piggy's bookish nature and are used as an important fire-starting tool.

The Signal Fire

The signal fire symbolizes the boys' connection to civilization. It is their first priority and their only hope of being rescued. As the story progresses, the fire dies down, symbolizing the boys' changing priorities and growing detachment from civilization.

The Lord of the Flies

The Lord of the Flies is an important symbol of ritualism, evil, and savagery. Placed on a stake as a peace offering to the beast, the pig's head shows the boys' detachment from reality. When Simon comes face to face with the Lord of the Flies during his hallucination, it becomes a symbol of the evil that has befallen the boys.

TEACHER NOTES

More

What Does the Beast Symbolize?

Assess the author's use of symbolism in the novel.

1. Choose a character from the chart and analyze what the beast represents to him. Which character is the least poignant example of this symbol in the novel? Which character is the best example of this symbol? Argue your opinions with clear reasons.
2. How is this symbol used or reflected in the novel's themes? Illustrate the ways in which the author's use of language deepens or weakens the meaning of the beast as a symbol. Explain and defend your ideas.

Weblink

The Complete Guide to Symbolism

Examine the blog post discussing the usage of symbolism in literature.

1. Compare and contrast examples of analytical descriptions of feelings and sensory descriptions using symbolism from the novel. Which kind is more effective in the novel? Provide reasons for your ideas.
2. Should analytical descriptions play a considerable role in the language of a novel? Why or why not?

EXTENSION ACTIVITY

Analyzing Bias in a Document

Students will analyze the bias that exists in a document from a different historical time and place, and how that bias shapes the opinions presented in the document. An exemplary analysis of bias in a document will meet the following criteria.

- Identifies the main points presented in the document
- Offers an in-depth interpretation of the document
- Differentiates between facts and opinions
- Identifies the writer
- Presents information about the writer
- Assesses the writer's reliability
- Determines the goals for the document
- Considers and assesses the writer's perspective
- Determines the writer's intended audience
- Identifies when and where the document was written
- Describes the historical context for the time and place in which the document was created, and analyzes how this context might have shaped the opinions expressed in the document
- Infers political or societal influences that may have shaped the opinions presented in the document
- Determines whether the writer had first-hand knowledge of the topic or event, or whether they are reporting as a secondary source
- Determines the document's bias
- Infers what interests the writer might have had that led them to create this document
- Explores other sources related to the topic of the document

The Use of Language

A major part of capturing the true nature of boys in *Lord of the Flies* is the author's use of language. The language used by children is very different from that used by adults, especially in the presence of other children. Golding uses language specific to each character in the dialogues he writes. The boys use **slang** commonly heard in English schools at the time. Their words come across as passionate and unrehearsed, recalling their unrestrained youth. Coming from different backgrounds and areas of England, some boys, such as Piggy, speak with distinct accents. These differences of language show not only geographical divisions, but class divisions as well, carried over from their former society.

Class Division

Two characters from obviously different backgrounds are Piggy and Jack. Piggy is an orphan, raised by his aunt who ran a candy store. This background shows that Piggy would have been part of the lower to middle class in wartime England. Although he is the most intellectual of the boys, he likely did not attend a well-regarded school. His accent is thick, unpolished, and **blue-collar**.

Jack, on the other hand, is the leader of the choir. He has traveled extensively outside of England and speaks in a "proper" accent. The reader can conclude that Jack likely comes from an upper-class family with military ties. He has probably attended exclusive schools and been given the best education available. Ralph comes from a similar background to Jack, his father being a military commander. These two become the natural leaders, while the lower-class, less fortunate Piggy becomes a target for the group's frustrations and aggression.

Civilization

"'I ought to be chief,' said Jack with simple arrogance, 'because I'm chapter chorister and head boy. I can sing C sharp.'

Another buzz.

'Well then,' said Jack, 'I–'

He hesitated. The dark boy, Roger, stirred at last and spoke up.

'Let's have a vote!'

'Yes!'

'Vote for a chief!'

'Let's vote –'

This toy of voting was almost as pleasing as the conch. Jack started to protest but the clamour changed from the general wish for a chief to an election by acclaim of Ralph himself. None of the boys could have found good reason for this; what intelligence had been shown was traceable to Piggy while the most obvious leader was Jack. But there was a stillness about Ralph as he sat that marked him out: there was his size, and attractive appearance; and most obscurely, yet most attractively, there was the conch."

Chapter One – The Sound of the Shell

Words and Phrases Used in *Lord of the Flies*

TEACHER NOTES

Document

William Golding - Nobel Lecture

Analyze the lecture given by William Golding at the Nobel Prize award ceremony in 1983.

1. In your opinion, what did Golding mean when he defined words as "a tool as primitive as the flint axe or even the soft copper chisel with which man first carved his own likeness in stone"? Defend your response with clear explanations.
2. What is the function of language, according to Golding? Support your response with excerpts from the novel.

Weblink

Literature's Emotional Lessons

Examine the article discussing emotional reactions to reading.

1. If Piggy's death scene were described using different language, would the student mentioned in the article have had the same emotional reaction? Why or why not?
2. Rewrite Piggy's death scene using different wording. How would this new version change the perception of the reader? How does language influence the emotional reaction of readers?

EXTENSION ACTIVITY

Writing a Book Review

Students will write a book review of the novel. An exemplary book review will meet the following criteria.

- Grabs the reader's attention with a creative headline
- Begins with an engaging lead to pull the reader into the article
- Introduces the title of the novel, the author, and the genre
- Provides a brief plot description that does not give away the entire story, and makes the reader want to learn more about the novel
- Supports arguments about the novel with accurate and detailed information
- Organizes the review and its arguments in a concise, clear, and logical manner
- Fits the format and style of a book review
- Follows the conventions of print or online journalism
- Demonstrates creativity in their approach
- Writes with a unique, engaging voice and perspective
- Provides fresh insight into the novel
- Provides an honest, authentic opinion on the novel
- Gives a clear recommendation on the novel, backed up by specific textual evidence
- Uses correct spelling, grammar, and punctuation

Impact of the Novel at the Time of Publishing

Golding began writing as a child and published his first work while he was still a student. However, this early beginning did not translate into an immediately successful writing career. While he continued writing throughout adulthood, Golding was unknown in the literary world. When he finally finished his first novel and began sending it out to publishers, he was in his forties. Golding was determined to publish the book despite the unenthusiastic reception it received.

Publication

The earliest promoter of Golding's book was an editor who had just begun working at the publishing house Faber and Faber. Charles Monteith worked with Golding to revise the book, including the original title, *Strangers from Within*. Monteith also worked hard to convince his bosses to publish the book.

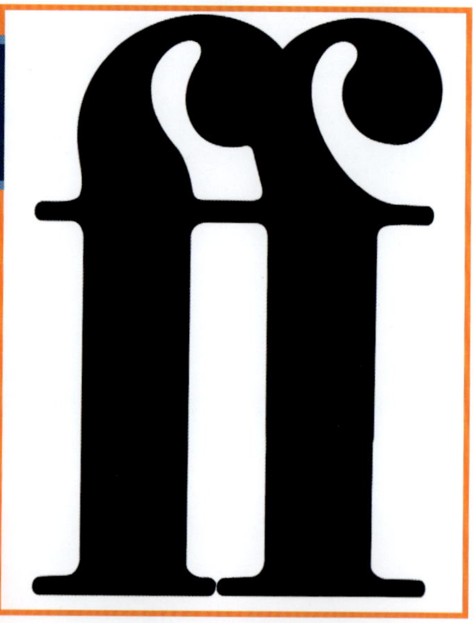

Spotlight

Lord of the Flies **was rejected by 21 different publishers** before finally being accepted.

The **initial print run** for *Lord of the Flies* was about **3,000 books**.

The **budget** for the **1963 *Lord of the Flies* film** is estimated to have been about **$250,000**.

Harsh Critiques

Publishers, critics, and reviewers who first read Golding's book were almost universal in their dislike of it. One rejection letter called the book "an absurd and uninteresting fantasy [...] rubbish and dull. Pointless." Golding's eventual publisher, Faber and Faber, even tried to keep news of the book hidden from its most famous advisor, T.S. Eliot. When the poet read *Lord of the Flies*, however, he called it a "splendid novel."

Initial Release

Upon its publication in 1954, the book was not an instant success. Its initial release was met with little excitement and harsh critiques, and not many copies were sold. However, a few years later, the popular British novelist E.M. Forster listed Lord of the Flies *as his "outstanding novel of the year." News of the novel spread and more copies began selling. Soon, it became required reading in schools around the world.*

Film Adaptation

In 1963, *Lord of the Flies* was adapted to the big screen by acclaimed British filmmaker, Peter Brook. The director used experimental filmmaking techniques, treating the film almost like a documentary. This approach gave the fictional story a lifelike, realistic look and feel. Much like the popular book it was based upon, the movie became critically acclaimed.

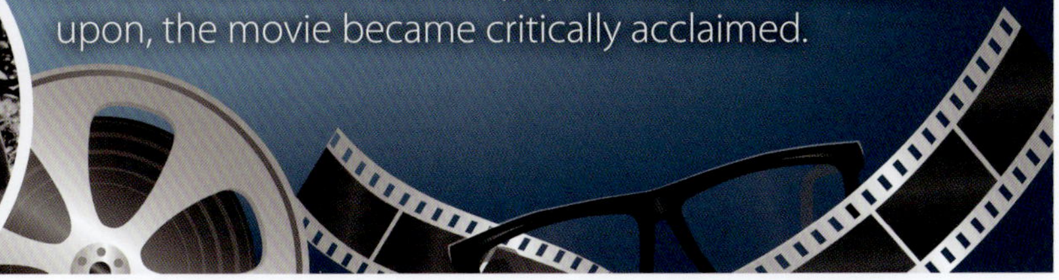

TEACHER NOTES

Document

Boys Will Be Boys

Examine Hollis Alpert's 1963 review of the film adaptation of the novel for *The Saturday Review*.

1. How is the relationship between the film adaptation and the novel described by the reviewer? Why did *Lord of the Flies* allow for such an adaptation? Sustain your opinion with evidence.
2. Why do you think that the film, despite being "a carbon copy" of *Lord of The Flies*, "doesn't reach the level of power and forcefulness obtained by the novel"? What could have made the tone of the film adaptation more faithful to the novel?

Video

Lord of the Flies **(original 1963 uncut, no subtitles) directed by Peter Brook**

Compare and contrast the assembly scene from the 1963 and 1990 film versions of the novel.

1. Think about the cinematography, pacing, and action in the scenes of the two films. Which of the film versions is more faithful to the tone of the novel? Are there aspects of either film scene that seem inconsistent or ineffective? Defend your ideas with well-reasoned evidence.
2. Which of the two actors playing Ralph is more effective? Which actor playing Piggy is the least effective? Provide thoughtful reasons for your responses.

EXTENSION ACTIVITY

Analyzing a Video

Students will watch and assess a video related to a component of the novel, and write an analysis of the video. An exemplary video analysis will meet the following criteria.

- Identifies the purpose of the video
- Identifies the intended audience of the video
- Describes how the content of the video is presented
- Summarizes the information and opinions presented in the video
- Analyzes the quality of the content presented in the video
- Assesses the effectiveness of the video
- Discusses the technical aspects of the video and whether or not these enhance the content
- Determines whether the images and graphics used in the video relate to the content
- Determines whether the video is easy to follow and understand
- Gives the analysis a clear and consistent purpose
- Organizes the analysis in a logical, effective manner
- Presents a strong, clear argument about the video
- Provides strong and accurate details to support the argument about the video
- Considers other perspectives on the purpose and effectiveness of the video
- Makes connections between the video and the novel
- Properly integrates quotations from the video
- Cites all sources used in the analysis

Impact of the Novel Now

Lord of the Flies remains one of the most popular novels in the English language. More than 60 years after its publication, it is still required reading in schools around the world. In addition to the students assigned to read the book, thousands of others read it for pleasure every year. Author Stephen King said it was "the first book with hands—strong ones that reached out of the pages and seized me by the throat. It said to me, 'This is not just entertainment; it's life-or-death.'"

Lord of the Flies has **sold** more than **25 million copies** in English alone, and even more worldwide.

The **1983 Nobel Prize** included an award of **1.5 million** Swedish krona. ($191,815 USD)

The **1990 *Lord of the Flies* film** made more than **$13 million** at the box office.

Nobel Prize

In 1983, Golding was awarded the Nobel Prize for Literature. After *Lord of the Flies*, he went on to write 11 more novels. While none reached the level of popularity of his first novel, they each made an impact on literature and society. The Nobel Committee chose Golding "for his novels which, with the **perspicuity** of realistic narrative art and the diversity and universality of myth, illuminate the human condition in the world of today."

Film Adaptation

In 1990, a second film version of *Lord of the Flies* was made. Director Harry Hook's adaptation modernized the story and changed several key details. In the film, the boys are American, not British. The film has been criticized for failing to capture the true meaning and emotion of both the book and the 1963 film.

Censorship

While the novel has been steadily popular for decades, it has also remained controversial and polarizing. Even today, *Lord of the Flies* faces challenges from critics, students, and parents. These challenges stem from the book's violent imagery and dark themes. In recent years, most challenges to the book have been denied, keeping it on library shelves and in the hands of students.

Parodies and Tributes

Lord of the Flies has become a part of popular culture. Its themes and imagery are instantly recognizable to millions of people around the world. The story has inspired music by bands such as Iron Maiden and U2. It has also been parodied and referenced in popular television shows such as *The Simpsons*, *Spongebob Squarepants*, *Seinfeld*, and *South Park*.

TEACHER NOTES

Video

The Simpsons - Das Bus

Analyze one of the parodies of *Lord of the Flies*.

1. How is *Lord of the Flies* adapted to fit a cartoon? How do the main features of Golding's characters correspond to the characters of *The Simpsons*? Why is this correspondence possible? Formulate some theories.
2. In your opinion, is the parody effective? Does its tone correspond to the tone of *Lord of the Flies*? Why or why not? What elements could be included to make this parody more effective?

Weblink

"Evans Library's Favorite Banned Books: *Lord of the Flies*"

Analyze the blog entry discussing the reasons *Lord of the Flies* has been banned, and why it should not have been, according to the blogger.

1. Why might school teachers' opinion about the themes discussed in the novel be valid? What arguments can be made against this opinion?
2. What reasons might Golding have had for including violent imagery and dark themes in the novel? Would the removal of these elements from the novel have any effect on the authenticity of the book, and if so, how?

EXTENSION ACTIVITY

Creating a Timeline

Students will explore a topic related to the novel and create a timeline to present their research on historical events connected to this topic. An exemplary timeline will meet the following criteria.

- Includes the most significant events pertaining to the topic to be compared and analyzed
- Includes interesting events
- Uses accurate information for all events, including date, location, and major details
- Orders the events in a chronological sequence
- Describes each event with accurate, vivid, and specific details
- Presents the topic from three or more perspectives
- Inspires the reader to ask thoughtful questions regarding the events and perspectives presented in the timeline
- Uses correct spelling, grammar, and punctuation
- Presents the timeline in a visually attractive and striking manner
- Presents the timeline in a neat, organized manner that is logical and easy to follow
- Uses creativity to present the timeline in an engaging manner
- Effectively communicates the historical information relating to the topic
- Supports each event with reliable sources
- Expresses a clear purpose for creating the timeline
- Enhances the reader's understanding of the topic
- Includes a correctly formatted bibliography of all sources used to create the timeline

Perspectives on Civilization

Golding was often described as a **pessimist**. The suffering and cruelty he witnessed in his life led him to focus on negative aspects of society and human nature. He viewed people as fundamentally greedy, jealous, and destructive. He did, however, have faith in humanity. Golding had also seen people act with cooperation, compassion, and charity. These positive human qualities are what create civilized societies.

Timeline of Civilization during Golding's Lifetime

December 14, 1911 Roald Amundsen of Norway becomes the first person to reach the South Pole.

June 28, 1914 Austria-Hungary's Archduke Franz Ferdinand is assassinated in Sarajevo. This is seen as the spark that ignited World War I.

1914-1918 World War I rages through Europe, the Middle East, and parts of Africa, killing about 8.5 million soldiers and 13 million civilians.

1900s

June 28, 1919 The Treaty of Versailles is signed, officially ending World War I. It also creates the League of Nations and severely punishes Germany for its role in the war.

August 27, 1928 Fifteen countries sign the Kellogg-Briand Pact, which is designed to make war illegal.

Lord of the Flies is an examination of civilization. Golding created a scenario in which he wrote about human nature in its most basic form. The innocent ignorance he had seen in groups of young boys inspired him. In his story, the boys become separated from civilization and struggle to maintain their own. They start their own society on the island, but ignorance, arrogance, and fear turn to violence and destruction. Golding perceived these same instincts in the leaders and societies that created two world wars during his lifetime.

1900s

October 29, 1929 The Great Depression begins when the stock market crashes and billions of dollars are lost in a single day.

January 30, 1933 Adolf Hitler is appointed Chancellor of Germany.

September 1, 1939 Germany attacks Poland, sparking World War II.

June 6, 1944 156,000 Allied troops, including William Golding, invade the French Coast at Normandy. Known as D-Day, this invasion would lead to Germany's eventual defeat.

February 9, 1946 Soviet dictator Josef Stalin makes a speech calling communism and capitalism "incompatible."

August 13, 1961 Communist powers in East Germany begin building the Berlin Wall.

The New York Times.

U.S. AND SOVIET REACH ACCORD ON CUBA; KENNEDY ACCEPTS KHRUSHCHEV PLEDGE TO REMOVE MISSILES UNDER U.N. WATCH

October 16, 1962 The Cuban Missile Crisis puts the world on the brink of nuclear war. It ends 13 days later, when Presidents Kennedy and Khrushchev come to a peaceful agreement.

1986 Oprah Winfrey becomes the first African American woman to host a nationally syndicated television show.

November 9, 1989 Crowds begin to chip away at the Berlin Wall as the border is officially opened between West Germany and East Germany.

TEACHER NOTES

Transparency–Timeline

Timeline of Civilization during Golding's Lifetime

Examine the historical, cultural, and contemporary contexts shown on the timeline. Then, contrast and correlate its elements with the themes and events presented in *Lord of the Flies*.

1. In what ways can historical events, culture, and social mores influence a population's perspective? How might these elements have shaped the way a reader in the 1950s would interpret the novel?
2. How might the era in which William Golding wrote *Lord of the Flies* have influenced the novel's themes and settings? Where in the novel is this most evident? Explain your reasoning.
3. Which current events, changes in laws, new ideas, or political discussions are shaping civilization today? How is it improving? In which ways is it not? Why?
4. How might current events and present perspectives affect the way a reader interprets the novel? Why is it important for readers to understand the era and context in which a novel is written?

EXTENSION ACTIVITY

Writing a Comparative Essay

Students will compare two literary devices used in the novel, and then write a comparative essay based on their analysis. An exemplary comparative essay will meet the following criteria.

- Consists of a one-paragraph introduction, three body paragraphs, and a one-paragraph conclusion
- Introduction includes an engaging lead statement about the topic of the essay, more detailed information about the novel, and a one-sentence thesis that specifically states the essay's argument
- Body paragraphs include a topic sentence that refers to the thesis and how the idea appears in the novel, a supporting sentence that points to this part of the novel, textual evidence of this idea from the novel, and analysis of this evidence
- Body paragraphs end with a transition to the next paragraph
- Conclusion refers to the topic of the essay and the three points presented in the body paragraphs, and restates the thesis
- Provides a thorough analysis of the literary devices in question
- Cites strong and thorough textual evidence to support analysis of what the novel says explicitly
- Presents a clear, specific thesis that indicates a high level of critical engagement
- Organizes ideas in a logical manner
- Communicates arguments in a clear, effective manner
- Properly integrates all quotations
- Correctly cites all sources used
- Correctly formats bibliography

Writing a Comparative Essay

The realistic and memorable characters in *Lord of the Flies* bring the story to life. Choose two characters from the book and make a list of their attributes. Compare and contrast the attributes of the two characters, and decide whether they are similar or different. Now, write an essay arguing your conclusion. Support your argument with logical reasoning and evidence from the novel.

How to Analyze and Compare Characters

Use the chart to guide your comparison of two characters in *Lord of the Flies*.

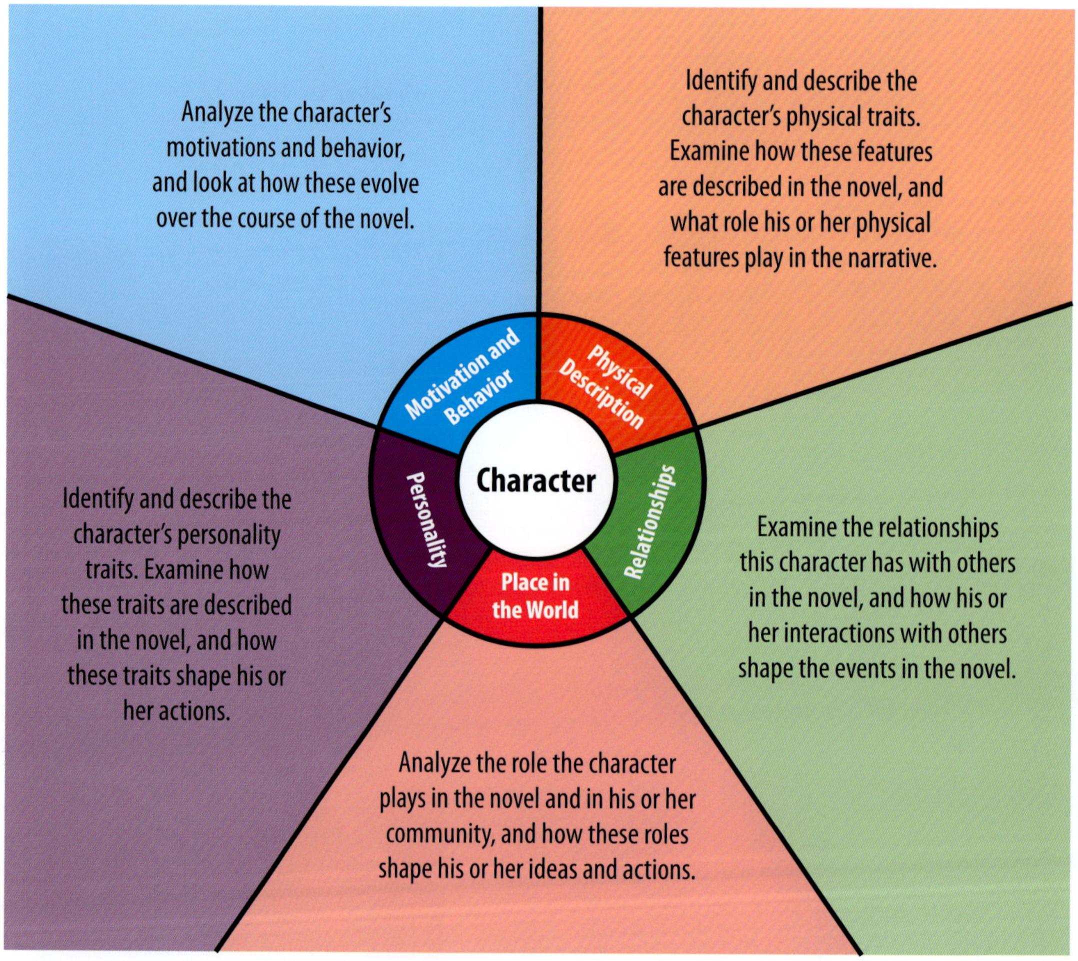

Comparing Ralph and Jack

Ralph

Personality
- Honest
- Confident
- Quiet

Place in the World
- 12-year-old English boy
- Marooned on an island

Motivation and Behavior
- Wants to survive and be rescued
- Fair
- Respectful
- Passionate

Relationships
- Chief of the tribe
- Believes his father, a commander in the Navy, will rescue them
- Has a pet pony at home
- Friends with Piggy, Simon, and Samneric

Physical Description
- Fair haired
- Athletic
- Strong
- Broad-shouldered
- Tall

Jack

Place in the World
- Early adolescent English boy
- Marooned on an island

Physical Description
- Skinny
- Red-haired
- Freckled
- "Ugly without silliness"

Motivation and Behavior
- Motivated by power
- Violent
- Savage
- Jealous

Relationships
- Lead boy of the choir
- Leader of the hunters
- Abusive towards Piggy
- Gives orders to Roger
- Becomes chief when the boys abandon Ralph

Personality
- Arrogant
- Angry
- Loud
- Manipulative

TEACHER NOTES

Transparency–Chart

Questions for Character Analysis

Analyze how specific character features, such as conflicts, motivations, relationships, place in the world, and personality affect the plot of *Lord of the Flies*. Cite strong and thorough textual evidence to support your analysis of what the novel says explicitly as well as the inferences you may have drawn from the novel's setting, themes, and symbols.

Quiz Answers

1. B
2. D
3. C
4. A
5. D
6. C
7. B
8. A
9. B
10. B

Key Words

authoritative: forceful in leadership

bastion: a stronghold or fortification

blue-collar: of the working class

charismatic: charming and confident

civilians: people who are not members of the military or police

Cold War: a state of political hostility between the American-led Western powers and the Soviet bloc countries

marooned: stranded on an island

militarism: a society with a strong military, ready for war

perspicuity: presented with a clear message

pessimist: someone with a negative outlook

ritualism: a fixed or traditional way of behaving

slang: informal language used by a particular group

suffragette: a woman seeking the right to vote through organized protest

uninhibited: without restraint or self-consciousness

Literary Terms

action: everything that occurs in a narrative

antagonist: the character who stands in opposition to the protagonist; in some cases, the antagonist creates or represents the conflict that the protagonist faces

character traits: aspects that make up a character's personality

climax: the most exciting or intense part of a story

coming of age: the process of growing up from youth to adulthood

dialogue: words spoken

dystopian: a setting or world lacking in freedom

exposition: the beginning of the story, where the characters and setting are introduced

falling action: the events that take place after the climax, leading up to the end of the story

Freytag's Pyramid: a narrative structure consisting of five elements; this includes exposition, rising action, climax, falling action, and resolution

imagery: a visual description

literary devices: unique structures of a literary work

literary elements: components of every literary work

motifs: major ideas in a literary work

narrative: a story

narrative structure: the way a story is built

narrator: the character or person telling the story, providing background information and opinions on the events, and connecting the gaps between major events and dialogue

plot: the specific action that propels a story forward

protagonist: the central character in a piece of fiction who must deal with a conflict and often undergoes some type of change as a result

resolution: the end of the story, when the problems are resolved and the action comes to a conclusion

rising action: the events that create increased drama or tension

style: the unique way that writers use language to tell their story; this can include word choice, the use of imagery, and the length and organization of sentences

symbolism: a stylistic device using symbols to represent and intensify concepts and ideas

theme: the underlying topic, idea, or position in a work that is often a general, universal statement about life

utopian: an idealistic, or nearly perfect setting

Index

LIGHTBOX

SUPPLEMENTARY RESOURCES

Click on the plus icon ⊕ found in the bottom left corner of each spread to open additional teacher resources.

- Download and print the book's quizzes and activities
- Access curriculum correlations
- Explore additional web applications that enhance the Lightbox experience

LIGHTBOX DIGITAL TITLES
Packed full of integrated media

VIDEOS

INTERACTIVE MAPS

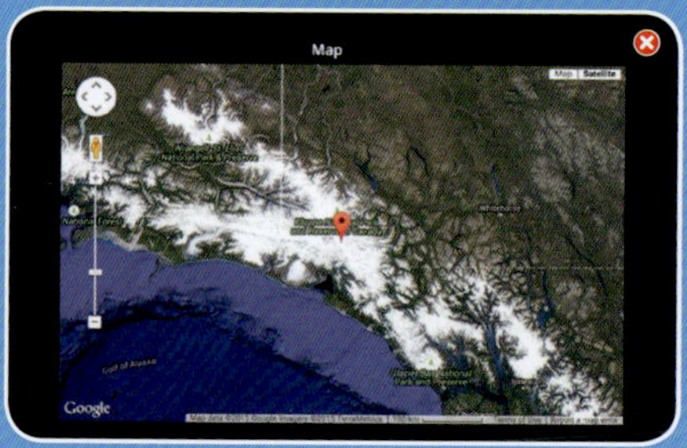

WEBLINKS

SLIDESHOWS

QUIZZES

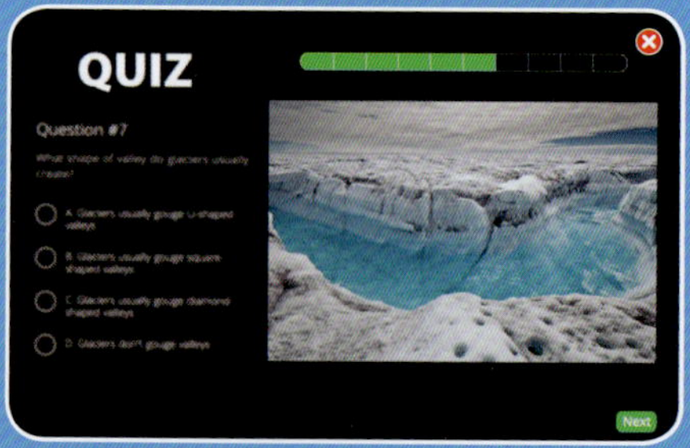

OPTIMIZED FOR
- ✓ TABLETS
- ✓ WHITEBOARDS
- ✓ COMPUTERS
- ✓ AND MUCH MORE!

Published by Smartbook Media Inc.
276 5th Avenue, Suite 704 #917
New York, NY 10001
Website: www.openlightbox.com

Library of Congress Cataloging-in-Publication Data

Names: Wiseman, Blaine, author.
Title: Lord of the flies / Blaine Wiseman.
Description: New York, NY : Smartbook Media, [2018] | Series: Lightbox literature studies | Includes index.
Identifiers: LCCN 2016056380 (print) | LCCN 2017015551 (ebook) | ISBN 9781510520004 (multi-user ebk.) | ISBN 9781510519992 (hard cover : alk. paper)
Subjects: LCSH: Golding, William, 1911-1993. Lord of the flies--Examinations--Study guides. | Airplane crash survival in literature. | Islands in literature. | Boys in literature.
Classification: LCC PR6013.O35 (ebook) | LCC PR6013.O35 L67 2018 (print) | DDC 823/.914--dc23
LC record available at https://lccn.loc.gov/2016056380

Printed in Guangzhou, China
2 3 4 5 6 7 8 9 0 26 25 24 23 22

062022
220610

Editor: Katie Gillespie
Art Director: Terry Paulhus

Every reasonable effort has been made to trace ownership and to obtain permission to reprint copyright material. The publisher would be pleased to have any errors or omissions brought to its attention so that they may be corrected in subsequent printings.

The publisher acknowledges Getty Images, Alamy, iStock, and Newscom as its primary image suppliers for this title.